THE
VAMPIRE
COMPETITION

Sink your teeth into
more Fang Gang stories . . .

My Vampire Grandad
The Headless Teacher
The Sweaty Yeti

THE
FANG GANG

THE
VAMPIRE SLAYING
COMPETITION

Roy Apps

Illustrated by
Sumiko Shimakata

BLOOMSBURY

For Lizzie Spratt – R.A.

To Yamai and all the well-behaved little
monsters of Goolish – S.S.

First published in Great Britain in 2007 by Bloomsbury Publishing Plc,

36 Soho Square, London, W1D 3QY

Text copyright © 2007 Roy Apps
Illustrations copyright © 2007 Sumiko Shimakata

A CIP catalogue record of this book is available from the British Library
ISBN 978 0 7475 8964 8

Printed and bound in Great Britain by Clays Ltd, St Ives Plc

1 3 5 7 9 10 8 6 4 2

All papers used by Bloomsbury Publishing are natural, recyclable products
made from wood grown in well-managed forests. The manufacturing processes
conform to the environmental regulations of the country of origin.

www.bloomsbury.com
www.fanggang.net

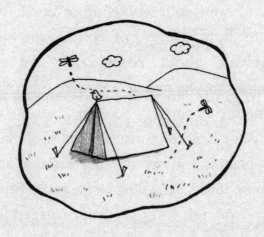

Chapter 1

I WOKE UP TO see the morning sunlight shining through the moth-eaten curtains on my bedroom window. I leapt out of bed with excitement. Today was the first day of the holidays and I was going to spend a few days camping with Grandad at Heemoglobin Castle!

Heemoglobin Castle was huge, haunted and creepy. It had a moat, a ruined chapel and a graveyard. It was said to be a place so scary, that at twelve o'clock on the night of the full moon, even your goosebumps come out in goosebumps. Unless, of course, you were a werewolf, ghoul, zombie or, like me, a vampire, in which case *you* were one of those doing the scaring.

It was going to be really good fun, I knew. I was planning to try out my vampire skill of turning into a bat. I'd had a go at the February full moon, but had only half managed it. Full moon, of course, is when your vampire skills are at their strongest.

As I ran downstairs to the kitchen, the smell of sizzling sausages filled my nostrils. Great! My favourite breakfast.

'Two sausages or three?' asked Grandad.

'Four, please,' I replied.

'You can have five if you like,' said Grandad, with a grin. 'I've got to use them all up before we go away.'

'You know, I'm really looking forward to going camping,' I said, through a mouthful of sausage.

'Are you, my boy? That's good,' replied
Grandad. There was a strange look about his
face and I should've realised then that he was
Up To Something. But I didn't. I was too busy
tucking into my sausages.

Half an hour later, I'd just finished packing
my rucksack when I heard a loud 'toot-toot'.
I looked out of the window and saw a
battered old minibus parked up by the front
gate. Millie Moon and her husband, Monty,

were going to give us a lift up to Heemoglobin Castle. They were Scarlet's great-uncle and aunt. Like me, Scarlet was a member of the Fang Gang. But she was a werewolf, whereas I was a vampire.

'Grandad!' I yelled. 'They're here!'

I rushed out of Drac's Cottage and down the front path to the minibus.

'Morning, Jonathan!' called Great-uncle Monty. 'Lovely weather for a spot of camping, isn't it?'

'Yes,' I agreed.

It was only then that I looked up at the windows in the back of the minibus. There, staring out at me, were the gruesome faces of twenty or so Goolish Brownies.

Great-aunt Millie, who was Brown Howl, was opening the back door. 'Move up, girls,' she ordered. 'Make room for Jonathan.'

'What . . . ?' I began.

'Morning, Jonathan,' said Great-aunt Millie, cheerfully, 'so glad you can join us at Brownie camp!'

Chapter 2

'BUT . . . I'M NOT going camping with the Brownies!' I protested in alarm. 'I'm going camping with Grandad.'

'That's right,' said Great-aunt Millie, smiling broadly.

'Grandad!' I called in terror, as I saw him slinking sneakily into the front of the minibus. 'Save me!'

But before I had a chance to run, Great-aunt

Millie and Uncle Monty had picked me up, lifted me into the back of the minibus and slammed the back doors.

It would've been bad enough going camping with a bunch of ordinary Brownies. But these weren't ordinary Brownies. They were the 1st Goolish Brownies. Ordinary Brownies are called things like elves and pixies; they like to sing and smile and make little old ladies cups of tea. Goolish Brownies are all banshees and goblins; they like to screech and swear and make sweet little old ladies cups of limp lizard leg and squashed beetle cocktail.

I lay on the floor of the minibus, twenty gruesome Brownies leering down at me. Suddenly, I saw a friendly face.

'Scarlet?'

'Hi, Jonathan!'

Scarlet was sitting in one of the back seats.

'Come and sit down and put your seat belt on,' said Scarlet. 'You look stupid lying there on the floor.'

'Are you going camping with the Brownies, too?' I asked her.

Scarlet sighed. 'I'm too old to be in the Brownies, of course, but my great-uncle and aunt won't let me stay in the house on my own. Usually, it's awful, but it'll be much better this year, with you there as an Honorary Brownie, too.'

'I don't want to be an Honorary Brownie,' I moaned.

'Don't be such a misery, Jonathan,' said Scarlet. 'You'll love it!'

As if to prove Scarlet wrong, a couple of sneaky faces popped up over the seats in front of us. They gave me toothy grins.

'Hi! You're Jonathan, aren't you? Mr Leech's grandson?' one of them asked me.

There was little point in denying it.

'You're a vampire, aren't you?'

I said I was.

'You do really gruesome scaring, don't you?'

I said I did.

'Will you teach us to do really gruesome scaring?' They flashed their blackened teeth at me.

I could hear Scarlet, next to me, snorting with laughter.

'I'm Zliva,' cackled the first Brownie, covering me in a mouthful of spit.

'And I'm Goblena,' said the other one.

'Of course Jonathan would love to teach you to be scary, wouldn't you, Jonathan?' said Scarlet, with a wicked grin.

Screeching with glee, Zliva and Goblena ducked back down into their seats.

'Oh, how sweet! They like you!' said Scarlet, with a giggle.

I shivered with terror as the ancient minibus echoed to the sound of twenty screeching and screaming Goolish Brownies.

Chapter 3

THE BROWNIE CAMPSITE at Heemoglobin Castle was in a field a little way from the ruined castle itself. In one corner were a couple of huts, where the Brownies would sleep. Through the hedge on the far side of the field was another field, which Scarlet said was sometimes used for touring caravans. We walked up the hedge and peered over, but it was empty. The Brownies were all running about screeching, looking for trouble.

Grandad was approaching us. 'Ah, there you are, Jonathan!' he said. 'Come and give us a hand putting up our tent!'

'Did you say *our* tent?'

'That's right, we'll be sharing! I'm going to make do without my coffin for a couple of nights.'

Three days and two nights of this torture. How would I stick it?

'When you said we were going camping,' I muttered, 'you didn't mention anything about Brownies!'

'Didn't I?' said Grandad, airily. 'Every year I go to Brownie camp. As their first aid helper.'

'You? A first aid helper?'

'Well, when I say first aid helper, I mean blood transfusion helper,' explained Grandad. 'You see, somebody has to be on hand for blood transfusions, and who better than a vampire? Why, vampires practically invented the whole idea of blood transfusions!'

'Brownies don't need blood transfusions, do they?' I asked.

'They certainly do,' replied Grandad. 'Especially after they've been in fights.'

I gulped.

There was only one hope: perhaps Mum and Dad would arrive home early. They were in the South Atlantic Ocean on a cruise. My gran had joined after she'd escaped from jail, where she'd been sent following an outburst of trolley rage in the local supermarket.

I took out the postcard I'd received from Dad just before we'd left for camp and read it again.

Caracas Airport, South America
Dear Jonathan,
Just to let you know that (finally!!!!) Mum, your gran and I are on our way home. Ant and Debs' penguin chicks have hatched. They are called Keith (named by Gran after your Grandad Leech) and Daisy (named by Mum after you). I know you're not called Daisy, but Mum said you would've been if you'd turned out to be a girl. Despite their strange habits, Ant and Debs are a nice enough couple as penguins go. I'm sure you'll enjoy having them and their chicks come to live with us. See you in a few days!
Love Dad

Jonathan Leech
Drac's Cottage
Goolish
England

P. S. Your gran's new lawyer has got her a free pardon!

Yes, perhaps later on that very day I'd look up and see Mum, Dad and Gran waving at me and calling, 'Jonathan, we've come to take you home!'

But, of course, I didn't. And in a way I was relieved. Part of me was looking forward to seeing them all again, but another part of me was dreading it. What would my dad think when he found out that I'd turned out like his father and grown up into a young vampire? What would it be like trying to live a vampire's life away from all my friends in the Fang Gang? What would it be like having to share my room with four penguins?

Lunch was disgusting: giblet jelly and sour cream. A great favourite of banshees and goblins, apparently. After lunch, I had a choice of helping wash up or going out with the Brownies to play 'Hide and Shriek'. I saw Zliva and Goblena flashing their menacing eyes at me and quickly decided on washing up. Scarlet offered to help me. There was tons of it. It took us almost until teatime.

After tea, Grandad got up and said, 'Right, everyone, it's story time!'

I was about to slink off, but Grandad called out, 'You can stay for this, too, Jonathan. You might learn something.'

'Sit next to us, Jonathan!' chorused Zliva and

Goblena. I sat down next to Scarlet.

'I will tell you something of the history of Heemoglobin Castle,' began Grandad. 'Although it was built a long, long time ago by the Earl of Heemoglobin, its most infamous resident owner was the earl's descendent, Dr Vlad Heemoglobin, a terrifying man whose name spelt terror to thousands of ordinary people.'

'Was he an evil vampire?' asked Zliva with glee.

'No,' said Grandad.

'A gruesome ghoul?' suggested Goblena.

'Worse than that,' said Grandad. 'Vlad Heemoglobin was a dentist!'

'Eeeik!' screeched the Brownies and even I shivered.

'But he was a good friend of Goolish's vampires,' explained Grandad. 'He kept their fangs sharp and shiny. And of course, in their turn, Goolish's vampires provided him with lots of business, so that he became a very rich man indeed. And now every year, on the night of the spring equinox, all the dark side folk have a Party-in-the-Graveyard. It takes place in the ruins of the chapel adjoining Vlad's haunted castle. A special party to bid a fond farewell to the lovely, long winter nights. This year's party is in two nights' time at the end of your camp.'

It sounded good fun: the Party-in-the-Graveyard. It also sounded a long way off. How would I ever survive two days of Brownie camp, let alone two nights of sharing a tent with Grandad?

That night I didn't get a lot of sleep. I don't know what was worse: Grandad asleep and snoring like a drain or Grandad awake and complaining that he was missing his coffin. So I sat up and made a new list:

Good stuff that will happen if I can survive the bad stuff that's happening now
1. Mum and Dad are coming home.
2. Party-in-the-Graveyard.

Bad stuff that's happening now
1. I'm at Brownie camp.
2. Grandad's at Brownie camp.
3. I'm sharing a tent with Grandad.
4. The Brownies *like* me!
5. I've had a girl penguin named after me.

Chapter 4

NEXT MORNING, THE Brownies went off to play a game of 'Murder' in the old graveyard up at the castle and Scarlet went with them. Grandad and Great-uncle Monty were busy trying to fix the Brownies' minibus, which had broken down, so I decided to go for a walk.

I made my way across the field until I came to the hedge. There was a little stile in the middle of it, so I climbed over and found myself in the other camping field. I gasped. The field had been empty the day before, but now there were half a dozen or so touring caravans parked up. They gleamed in the afternoon sun. All of them had satellite dishes on their roofs and most of them had smart 4x4s parked alongside.

Suddenly, I heard a voice behind me yell: 'Zeus! Come *here*, boy!' I turned round just in time to see a dog bounding towards me, all four legs off the ground. Before I could move out of the way, the dog had knocked me sideways. I fell to the ground and the dog landed on top of me.

'Zeus! Come here!' ordered the voice, again.

But Zeus didn't come. Instead, I felt his hot breath on my face as I used my full vampire strength to roll out from under the grip of his hairy paws.

I got up and took a long, hard look at Zeus's owner, who by now had managed to get a choke chain around the dog's neck. He was a boy about my age, I suppose.

'Sorry about that,' he said.

'I suppose you're going to say "he doesn't mean any harm, he's quite friendly really",' I replied, sarcastically.

'No, I was going to say he's a real killer. If you hadn't rolled off him like that he would probably have had your ear off if not your arm.' He turned to the dog. 'You're a naughty boy, Zeus!' he said. 'I'm Troy by the way. Sorry

I can't shake your hand but I need both of them to hold on to Zeus's lead.'

'I'm Jonathan,' I said.

'Which is your caravan?' asked Troy.

'None of them,' I replied. 'I'm with the Brown . . . Er . . . I live not far from here. In Goolish.'

'Right,' said Troy. 'Zeus is taking me for a walk; do you want to join us?'

'Yeah, OK,' I said. Anything to put some more distance between me and the Brownies.

Zeus took us across the caravan field and through a gap in the hedge on the far side. Then we went through a wood and came out close to Heemoglobin Castle.

'That looks one scary place,' commented Troy.

'Its most famous resident was Dr Vlad Heemoglobin, a dentist,' I explained.

Troy shivered. 'No wonder it looks so creepy. What are those girls up to in the grave-yard? They all look as if they're trying to murder each other.'

With a bit of luck, they might succeed, I thought.

Even Zeus seemed a bit unsettled by the sight of Heemoglobin Castle − or possibly the Brownies − and he started tugging at Troy. We made our way back to the caravan field.

'Which is your caravan?' I asked Troy.

'That one,' he replied, pointing to a gleaming silver trailer the size of an aircraft hangar with all sorts of aerials sticking out of the roof. 'It's got satellite telly, Wi-Fi, the lot. It belongs to my parents' friends, Vera and Roderick. The Stoats. I'm staying with them because Mum and Dad have gone to a conference. They're both teachers.'

'Oh, I'm sorry,' I said. I felt for the guy. I mean, it's bad enough I thought, having to put up with teachers at school. Imagine having to live with a couple of them!

Troy shrugged. 'It could be worse. At least they're not like Vera and Roderick.'

'Aren't they teachers, too, then?'

'Oh no!' muttered Troy. 'They're . . . well,

you'll never guess. Tell you what, come round to the caravan and you'll get a clue.'

'There,' said Troy, pointing. Hanging down inside the windows were lots of colourful little flags and pennants.

'*European Vampire Slayers International Meet: Transylvania 2005,*' read one. '*All England Vampire Slayers Conference 2004,*' read another.

'Worked it out yet?' asked Troy. 'Vera and Roderick Stoat are vampire slayers.'

Chapter 5

MY MOUTH WENT completely dry. I couldn't speak.

'I can understand you being speechless,' sighed Troy. 'I mean, can you imagine anything more embarrassing?'

Suddenly, an ear-piercing shriek caught our ears. We quickly turned around.

'It's those girls!' he whispered. 'They're letting the tyres down on next door's caravan! Come on!'

Troy ran towards the noise, followed by Zeus, who had started barking like mad. As I peered carefully round the corner of Troy's caravan I could see Zliva, Goblena and a couple of the other Brownies by the wheels of the neighbouring vehicle. The last thing I wanted was for Zliva and Goblena to see me and start yelling my name.

I needn't have worried. As soon as they saw Zeus bounding towards them, they scampered away down the field.

Troy and Zeus came back.

'Cheek!' he said.

I nodded. 'Anyway, I'd best be getting home,' I said.

I left Troy in his caravan and wandered back down to the Brownies' campsite. I found Scarlet helping her Great-uncle Monty get the black pudding ready for lunch.

'Are you all right, Jonathan?' she asked.

I shook my head. 'I'm calling an Emergency Meeting of the Fang Gang.'

'But there's only two of us here,' Scarlet pointed out.

'That'll do,' I muttered, darkly.

As soon as Scarlet had finished helping Great-uncle Monty, we went round the back of the hut and I told her all about Troy and the vampire-slaying Vera and Roderick Stoat.

'We'd better tell Great-aunt Millie, Great-uncle Monty and your grandad,' said Scarlet.

It was teatime before we managed to get to talk to them.

'Well, you just make sure you keep out of the way of these Stoat people,' said Grandad. 'You know what vampire slayers are like.'

'Of course I know what vampire slayers are like,' I retorted, crossly. 'They slay vampires!'

'Don't you think we should do something?' suggested Scarlet.

'We're far too busy looking after the Brownies to be bothered with vampire slayers,' said Great-aunt Millie. It was all right for her, she wasn't a vampire, she was a werewolf.

'Grandad?' I asked.

'I've got to be on duty in case anyone needs a blood transfusion,' said Grandad. 'Besides, I've got to teach the Brownies their songs. Would you believe that none of them know the proper dark-side words to "Mary Had a Little Lamb"?'

'And we've only got one day left to get ready for the Party-in-the-Graveyard,' said Great-uncle Monty. 'It's all go, go, go.'

After tea, Scarlet and I went and sat at the back of the hut.

'Typical,' said Scarlet, crossly. 'I might've guessed they wouldn't take us seriously. Do you know what worries me?'

I shook my head.

'The fact that these two vampire slayers should have turned up here at this time of year,' she said.

'Do you think they know about the Party-in-the-Graveyard?'

'They might. Every dark-side creature from miles around is going to be there after all,' said Scarlet.

'So, safety in numbers,' I reasoned. 'And surely, the night of the full moon is when all creatures of the night are at their strongest?'

Scarlet shook her head. 'You're missing the point, Jonathan. They may be at their strongest, but they're also at their most vulnerable. After a couple of glasses of vintage blood, none of the adult vampires will be in a fit state to fight off vampire slayers. And the ghouls, werewolves and zombies won't be much better. Not that the zombies are ever any use, anyway.'

In the growing darkness we could just make out a thin wisp of smoke curling up from the Brownies' campfire as they all sang what Grandad called 'the proper darkside words' to 'Mary Had a Little Lamb'.

Mary had a little lamb
She had it with mint sauce
Potatoes, peas and gravy
And a glass of blood, of course.

Scarlet turned to me. 'There's only one thing for it. We'll have to get back down into Goolish and warn the rest of the Fang Gang.'

Chapter 6

NEXT MORNING, while the Brownies were having their breakfast of shredded gristle and brawn flakes, Great-uncle Monty announced that while Grandad and Great-aunt Millie took the Brownies out on a Poisonous Toadstool Hunt, he was going down into Goolish to fetch supplies and equipment for the Party-in-the-Graveyard.

'Can Jonathan and I come with you?' asked Scarlet.

'Of course,' said Great-uncle Monty.

So, about mid-morning, Great-uncle Monty dropped us off in the supermarket car park.

We called on Griselda first of all.

'Oh my,' she exclaimed, 'you two *do* look gloomy. What's up?'

We told her all about Troy and Vera and Roderick Stoat at the caravan park. Griselda looked worried.

'I'll get Gory and Crombie,' she said. 'Headquarters in ten.'

And with that, she fluttered into her bat form and flew out through the open window.

Ten minutes later, we were all in the Fang Gang headquarters; the gravedigger's hut on the far side of the churchyard. Scarlet and I told our story again, for the benefit of Gory and Crombie.

When we had finished, Gory yawned and said: 'So? Two old vampire slayers are parked up at the caravan site. That's no big deal, is it?'

'It's the Party-in-the-Graveyard tonight,' said Scarlet.

'We know that,' replied Gory. 'So what? There are two of them and dozens of us vampires, werewolves, ghouls and zombies.'

'That's right, man,' agreed Crombie the Zombie. 'I mean, we've lived in Goolish all this time with Tiffany and Mrs Bliss and they've not actually done any slaying, have they?'

Tiffany was in our class at school. She reckoned she was a big shot vampire slayer and had once started a Stake 'n' Brussels Sprouts Club to prove it. It had originally been called The Stake 'n' Garlic Club, until I had suggested that Brussels sprouts had a worse stink than garlic. It had only ever had two members; Tiffany herself and me, and I was only in it because I was a spy from the Fang Gang.

'And that's another thing,' I said. 'The last week of term, Tiffany was definitely looking *smug* about something.'

'She *always* looks smug, man,' Crombie pointed out.

'No,' I said. 'This was a *different* sort of smug look. Like she *knew* something.'

'You told us the other week that Tiffany and her mum had given up vampire slaying,' Gory growled.

'That's what she *said*,' I mumbled. 'But supposing she was lying?'

'You've got Tiffany Bliss on the brain,' snapped Gory. 'As to these Stoat people, we don't even know that they're aware there's a Party-in-the-Graveyard up at the castle tonight.'

He had a point. Supposing it was just coincidence that the Stoats had chosen Heemoglobin Castle for their weekend away?

'I'm busy enough as it is,' said Griselda. 'I still haven't bought a frock for tonight and my mum's promised to straighten my hair when she gets back from having her nails done.'

'Look, Jonathan, why don't you go and see your friend Troy again and get him to tell you a bit more about these Stoat people?' suggested Gory.

'I'm not sure that he will,' I said. 'He seemed to be a bit embarrassed about staying with a couple of vampire slayers.'

'Then you'll just have to try bullying or torturing him, won't you?' said Gory.

I gulped. 'Bullying or torture . . . ?'

'Whatever it takes. I mean, you and Scarlet are the ones who seem to think we're all in mortal danger. All those in favour of Jonathan paying a visit to Troy and torturing him if necessary, raise your hands.'

Everyone – including Scarlet – put up their hands.

'Right, that's that decided,' said Griselda.

We left the hut and walked out into the churchyard. I was still worried. But things could have been worse. At least no one had asked Scarlet and me just what *we* were doing hanging about up at Heemoglobin Castle.

If I'd had to tell them I was at Brownie camp, I would've died of shame.

Chapter 7

SCARLET AND I left Gory, Griselda and Crombie in town and went off to the supermarket car park.

The Brownies' minibus was no longer there.

'I don't believe it,' muttered Scarlet. 'Monty's gone back to the campsite without us!'

'We'll just have to walk back,' I sighed.

'But it's miles!' groaned Scarlet.

We'd just started to climb the hill out of

Goolish and Scarlet was getting grumpier by the minute, when a smart 4x4 sped past us, screeched to a halt and then reversed back.

The rear window wound down and there was Troy, grinning at me.

'Hi, Jonathan,' he said, 'do you want a lift?'

'Yes, please!' called Scarlet, and before I had time to draw breath, she'd opened the door and leapt in next to Troy.

She hadn't seen what I had seen in the back of the car: Zeus.

'Careful! The dog!' Troy and I yelled together.

But Zeus didn't appear to be interested in tearing Scarlet limb from limb. He whimpered, gave a playful little bark and held out his paw for Scarlet to shake.

'Hello!' said Scarlet.

'Woof!' said Zeus.

'Aren't you going to introduce us, Troy, dear?' asked a steely-eyed woman in the passenger seat who I took to be Mrs Stoat aka Vera the Vampire Slayer.

'Er . . . this is Jonathan,' said Troy. 'I met him up at the caravan site, yesterday. Jonathan, these are my parents' friends Mr and Mrs Stoat.'

'I'm Scarlet,' said Scarlet, before I had a chance to introduce her.

'Woof,' said Zeus.

'And that's Zeus,' I said, gingerly slipping in next to Scarlet. But Zeus wasn't interested in me. He was giving Scarlet his undivided attention.

We pulled away up the hill and Mr and Mrs Stoat started chatting to each other.

'It was so nice of her to invite us to her house for morning coffee, wasn't it Roderick?' said Mrs Stoat.

Roderick nodded.

'She was quite, quite wonderful, wasn't she, Roderick?' said Mrs Stoat.

'Oh yes. Quite wonderful,' agreed Roderick. 'So determined to fight the forces of evil.'

'And her daughter, too. So charming, so polite. She'd make a super little friend for you, Troy.'

Troy didn't say anything but I fancied I heard a kind of painful, strangled cry coming from his throat.

'What was her name? Tuppenny?'

'Tiffany,' said Roderick.

I heard another painful, strangled cry.

This time it came from *my* throat.

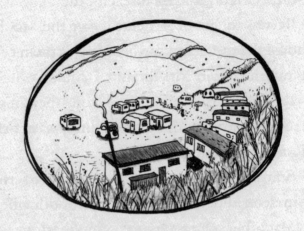

Chapter 8

I F MRS BLISS AND Tiffany were friends with the Stoats, it could mean only one thing: despite what Tiffany had told me, she and her mother were still into vampire slaying.

We got to the caravan site and piled out of the 4x4.

As I walked away down the field with Scarlet, Zeus seemed very reluctant to leave her side.

'See you, Troy,' I said.

'Yeah, right,' he replied.

I tried to get some clue from the way he looked at me as to whether his was the face of a vampire slayer or not, but I couldn't. Just a kind of weary smile. Mind you, spending a couple of hours with Tiffany Bliss was enough to make anyone feel weary.

Scarlet and I didn't say anything to each other on the way down to the bottom field. We both had too much going on in our minds.

We found the Brownie camp deserted.

'I guess Great-aunt Millie is out with the Brownies,' said Scarlet. 'And no doubt Great-uncle Monty and your grandad are up at the castle getting things ready for tonight.'

We walked up to the hedge and stared into the caravan field.

'You've got to do something,' said Scarlet.

At that moment, I saw Vera and Roderick walking away from their caravan, Zeus at their heels.

Without a word, I clambered over the stile and keeping my eyes peeled all the time, made my way across to the Stoats' caravan. I knocked on the door. No answer. Supposing Troy was out as well and we'd just not seen him go? I put my hand on the handle and pushed down. It was locked. If I could get in and have a look around, I might be able to

find out just what the Stoats had got in mind in the way of vampire slaying, without the tedious business of having to pump Troy for the information. But how to get in?

'It's a pity Gory isn't with us, he could have shimmered in.'

I spun round and saw Scarlet standing there, a grim smile on her face.

'What do you want?' I snapped. 'You made me jump!'

'I just came to point out that you were wrong when you said it was all down to you. It's not.'

'Oh no?'

'No, Jonathan.' Scarlet's face was serious. 'It's down to *us*. Now, one of those big front windows is open and on the latch. If we open it some more you'll be able to squeeze in.'

'And you?'

'I'll keep guard. If I see anything, I'll howl.'

'I am quite able to look after myself you know,' I said. 'I *am* a vampire.'

'And behind every good vampire there is an

equally good werewolf,' said Scarlet. 'Now shut up and get over to that window.'

The window opened without a problem. I eased myself up on to the ledge, Scarlet gave me an almighty shove from behind and the next moment I was flat on my face on the floor of the Stoats' caravan.

Chapter 9

I WAS IN THE SITTING-ROOM area. It was spotlessly clean. Brown, plumped-up cushions lay scattered on the beige window seats. I wasn't sure what I was looking for, but whatever it was I wouldn't find it in this room.

I went through to the middle area of the caravan, where the kitchen was. This was spotlessly clean, too. The stainless-steel sink sparkled and two tea towels hung neatly on a small rail by the door. On the worktop, though, was a small sheaf of papers stapled together. I looked at the top sheet. *Vampire Slaying in Goolish*, it read. I turned it over and was about to start to read the document when suddenly, I felt an arm around my throat.

It took me completely by surprise. I lost my footing and fell backwards on to my attacker. We were on the floor in no time, but by then

I was already beginning to summon up my vampire strength. I pulled the arm away from my neck. Still holding on to it I turned myself over and found myself looking into Troy's face.

'What are you doing, jumping on me like that?' I asked him, crossly.

'I thought you were a burglar,' muttered Troy.

'Do I look like a burglar?'

'From where I'm sitting, yes,' said Troy, with a wince. 'You broke into Vera and Roderick's caravan and I caught you snooping about. Look, would you mind getting off me? You're quite strong, you know.'

'Oh, I know,' I said, stepping away and sitting on the kitchen floor with my back to the sink.

Troy sat up, too, facing me. 'You'd only got to knock, you know,' he said, gruffly, 'I would've let you in.'

'Sorry.' I shrugged. 'It's all a bit silly, really. You see . . . I had this dare with a mate that I could break into a caravan.'

'What mate?'

'Er . . . Scarlet. You met Scarlet. In the car?'

'Liar,' said Troy.

'Who are you calling a liar?' I growled.

'You,' replied Troy. 'It's to do with vampire slaying, isn't it?'

'Vampire slaying? Why should I be interested in vampire slaying?' I tried to sound as bored as I could.

'Why else would you have been reading Roderick's vampire-slaying brochure on the worktop there?'

How much did Troy know about me or the dark side of Goolish and what did he think about vampires and other creatures from the dark side? I didn't know. I had to be careful. Very careful.

Troy looked at me, steadily. 'So, come on, why are you interested in vampire slaying? So interested in fact, that you'd break into a stranger's caravan?'

Should I dare trust this boy from the light side and tell him the truth? Or should I do what Gory had suggested and bully him and torture him until he told me all he knew? I could already feel my heart beating loudly. The louder it beat the more adrenalin it pumped round my body – and with the adrenalin came that vampire strength to my arms and legs.

All I had to do was to reach out and grab Troy's wrist, twist his arm behind his back and . . .

Chapter 10

BUT I DIDN'T.

Gory would have gone for him, I knew. But I couldn't. If Troy wasn't a vampire slayer already, then bullying him and hurting him would surely turn him into one for the rest of his life. No, I had to take a chance and trust him with the truth. At least, with *some* of the truth.

I started to tell Troy all about Goolish and its

residents. 'Well, it's like this,' I began. 'They're not bad. At least, they're no worse than people from the light side. They are simply, well . . . *different*. And I will do anything I can to make sure that none of them get slain.'

'Anything?'

I held his look. 'Anything,' I repeated. 'Which is why when Vera said you'd been to see Mrs Bliss and Tiffany, I had to find out just what was going on.' I paused. 'And I thought breaking in and finding out stuff for myself might be easier than trying to get it out of you.'

'You didn't trust me?'

'I wasn't sure,' I replied.

'I see,' said Troy. 'But you're trusting me now, telling me you're a friend of these creatures?'

I nodded.

Troy looked hard at me. 'I knew, anyway.'

'How?'

'Tiffany told me,' said Troy.

'Did she now?' I said. *That must mean she hasn't twigged that I am a vampire*, I thought.

'She said you were very easily led astray, particularly by a group of gross kids who call themselves the Fang Gang,' he added.

'Oh?'

'Mind you, I didn't believe her.' He laughed. 'Tiffany believes that the Fang Gang are all from the dark side.'

I nodded.

'And you're just their friend?'

I nodded again.

'I think Tiffany's got it wrong,' said Troy, quietly. 'I think you're a vampire, too.'

'Don't be daft!' I said, tensing myself for trouble. 'Do I look like a young vampire?'

'Give it a few hours,' Troy said. 'The way you floored me just now. That wasn't the strength of a kid my age, a kid smaller than me.'

So, I'd given myself away. I was *that* angry. 'I could floor you again, you know!' I said, starting to get up.

'I know,' said Troy.

But I didn't. I sat down again.

'I'm surprised you didn't turn yourself into a bat and fly in through the open window. I probably wouldn't have seen you.'

'I can't turn into a bat, properly,' I mumbled. 'Not yet. Next full moon, maybe. If I get a chance.'

'Don't worry, Jonathan, I'm on your side.' Troy's look was serious.

'Tell me, then,' I said. 'What kind of vampire-slaying plans do the Stoats and Blisses have?'

'It's not just Vera and Roderick and Tiffany and her mum,' said Troy. 'There are vampire slayers in every caravan on this site.'

'What! How come they've homed in on Goolish?' I asked.

'Apparently, Vera and Roderick met Mrs Bliss when they were on holiday in Transylvania,' Troy explained. 'They cooked up this idea for the biggest vampire-slaying event of the year. Mrs Bliss has even arranged for a TV crew to be here.'

'And what event's that?' I asked.

'The Goolish Grand Vampire Slaying Competition,' replied Troy.

'The *what*?' I exclaimed.

Suddenly, I heard an urgent howling from outside. Scarlet's warning! But before I had time to do anything, there was the sound of voices from outside the door.

'Quick!' whispered Troy, grabbing my arm. 'In here!'

He hauled me through into a small compartment, hardly bigger than a cupboard. 'This is my bedroom,' he said. 'You stay in here. Then you'll be able to hear everything. They're about to hold a Vampire Slaying Competition Planning Meeting.'

'Troy?' called Vera. 'We're back, dear! Hurry along!'

'Coming!' called Troy. And with that, he slipped out of the compartment, leaving the door slightly ajar.

Chapter 11

'I DECLARE THIS meeting of vampire slayers open,' boomed Vera Stoat's voice. There was a pause and then they all began to chant:

'Silver bullet; clove of garlic
Weapons of our ancient art
We won't rest until we've hammered
Stakes through every vampire's heart.'

'It's my pleasure to report on a very successful

meeting that Roderick and I had with Belinda Bliss this morning, to firm up details of tonight's vampire-slaying competition,' Vera Stoat went on. 'As you know, Belinda has spent many years in television, exposing scandals and outrages up and down the country—'

A loud cough interrupted the Stoat speech.

'Excuse me, Vera.' It was a plummy man's voice which spoke. 'But are you sure the details of meetings such as this are suitable for the ears of a young man such as Troy here?'

'Before our visit to Belinda Bliss this morning, I would have undoubtedly said no,' replied Vera. She paused. 'What I am going to tell you may come as a shock. Even to those of you who witnessed the appalling activities in Transylvania at last year's vampire-slaying competition. However, according to Belinda Bliss, the most dangerous creatures from the dark side in Goolish are actually children! Some of them as young as ten or eleven.'

A gasp of horror went round the room.

'But, my dear Vera, that simply is appalling!' gushed the plummy voice which had asked the question.

'Indeed, Cyril, it is. But now you understand why I locked young Troy in the caravan. We just can't be too careful.'

There was a murmur of agreement.

'And you can also understand why I have asked Troy to join us for this meeting. He and young Tiffany could be incredibly helpful in slaying some of the younger vampires for us.'

'Excuse me? But who is this Tiffany?' asked another member of the meeting.

'Belinda Bliss's young daughter,' explained Vera. 'She's a most delightful girl, isn't she, Troy?'

There was no response from Troy.

'Indeed,' Vera went on, 'it was young Tiffany who first alerted her mother to the presence of vampires and other creatures from the dark side in the otherwise delightful seaside town of Goolish.'

I was so riveted, so horrified by what they

were talking about that I'd not heard the pad of small footsteps coming up the corridor. Suddenly I heard a long, low growl. I looked down into Zeus's snarling jaws.

'Zeus!' I heard Troy cry, before I managed to slam the door to.

Zeus growled and barked and pawed at the door.

'Zeus! Come here, boy!' I heard Troy's voice outside the door as he struggled to get the chain round the dog's neck.

Then I heard Vera approaching. 'Honestly, Troy, that dog is completely bonkers,' she snapped. 'Take him outside.'

I waited until the footsteps disappeared, then I pushed the door open a crack. Roderick had taken over the meeting now.

'The most exciting thing,' he was saying, 'is that Belinda Bliss has arranged for there to be television coverage of our delightful vampire-slaying competition. For the first time ever, the whole country will be able to see these dark-side creatures in their true hideousness. Who knows, vampire slaying may soon become as popular a hobby as bowls or trainspotting. The other exciting thing is that Belinda Bliss has donated the "Bliss Cup" to the person who manages to slay the most vampires.'

A round of applause and a whoop of excitement greeted this news.

'Right, everybody!' Vera's voice rose above the cheering. 'We all still have much to do before tonight's exciting event. Unless there is any other business, I declare this meeting closed.'

There was more chatter and murmur. I could just make out flashes of colour as the various vampire slayers left the caravan.

Then Vera said, 'Come along, then, Roderick!'

I heard the Stoats go out. Then the door slammed and the key turned in the lock.

I edged the door open a little further and saw that I was completely alone in the caravan. Keeping close to the floor, so that I couldn't be seen, I crept through the sitting-room area. Through the large front window I could see Roderick, Vera and Troy and one or two other people.

I wasn't going to take any chances, not with this lot of vampire slayers around. I would wait until the coast was completely clear before I slipped out of the window to safety.

I crept back into the bedroom compartment. Almost immediately I felt a shudder and a rumble. The caravan was moving!

Chapter 12

THE CARAVAN ROCKED and bumped over the field. I slithered around the floor, then grabbed hold of a post holding up the bunk beds to try and steady myself. I pulled myself up until I could just see out of the window.

We headed out of the campsite then down the hill towards Goolish. As we drove along the seafront I peered out of the window at the grey sea. We turned off the front and started heading towards the far side of town. We were just passing the shopping centre when the caravan suddenly jolted, throwing me across the floor. We had come to a stop. I wasn't going to risk climbing out through the window, though; it was far too easy for Roderick to see me in the wing mirror. I heard one of the car doors slam and then a voice:

'Thank you ever so much for the lift, Mrs Stoat.' Through the window I could just see a small, dark figure giving a little wave to the Stoats, Troy and, no doubt, Zeus. It was Scarlet!

As we pulled away, Scarlet's face passed by my window and she gave me a little smile. Honestly! She was meant to be my friend, and here she was smiling away as I was being driven off into the unknown by a couple of vampire slayers!

We reached the smart houses on the edge of town. There was only one family I knew who lived up here: the Blisses. We pulled up outside their house. I heard the passenger door slam and Vera shouting:

'Steady, Roderick! Left a bit, no, too much . . . too much!'

Roderick was trying to reverse the caravan into the Blisses' front drive. There was a bump as we hit a gatepost.

'Steady . . . full lock . . . full lock . . . No, the other way!'

There was another bump as we hit the other gatepost. It took another fifteen minutes for Roderick to get the caravan into the Blisses' front drive. He might be ace at vampire slaying, I thought, but he's absolute rubbish at reversing a caravan.

More car doors slammed and then all went quiet. It was time to make good my escape. I went through to the sitting-room area and looked out of the window. The coast seemed to be clear. Provided no one was looking out of the Blisses' front window, I should be safe. I started to undo the latch when I heard a rustling sound behind me. I spun round and saw a tall ghostly figure shimmering through the wall towards me. It was Gory!

'Aargh!' he yelled. 'Help!'

'Hello, Gory,' I said. 'What are you doing here?'

'Me? I like that! What are *you* doing here?' he demanded to know. 'You gave me the shock of my life. I thought the caravan was empty. Griselda, Crombie and I have been

keeping a watch on the Blisses' place and I thought I'd come and have a nose around this caravan, see what it was all about.'

'So, you finally decided to take my advice about Tiffany being up to something, then, did you?' I asked.

Before Gory could answer, we heard the caravan door open behind us and in came Troy – and Zeus, who growled, menacingly.

'This is Gory,' I told Troy. 'Gory, this is Troy.'

'Grrr . . .' growled Zeus.

'Oh, and this is Zeus.'

'Er . . . is he friendly?' Gory asked Troy in a terrified voice.

'No,' said Troy. He looked Gory up and down. 'Are you one of the Fang Gang? Like a ghost or something?'

'Ghost? I'm a ghoul actually,' replied Gory, angrily, before realising what he'd actually said. He checked himself. 'Hey, who told you all about the Fang Gang?'

'Let's get out of here, shall we?' said Troy. 'While the coast is clear. They're all out in the back garden at the moment, sharpening stakes.'

I shivered and followed Zeus and Troy down the steps of the caravan and out on to the front drive.

Chapter 13

WE'D ONLY JUST reached the pavement when Zeus began pulling Troy along, barking and sniffing the ground. The house next door had a big hedge in front of it. Zeus dived in, barking excitedly.

'Hello, Zeus!' said a voice from the hedge. Out came Scarlet. 'Hi, guys!' she said, busily patting Zeus, who was wagging his tail. 'I came up here as quickly as I could. I thought

you might need rescuing, Jonathan, but I see Troy got to you first.'

'Hold on a moment,' growled Gory. 'There's something you ought to know. We have a traitor in the camp.' He shot me a filthy look. 'Jonathan's being telling Troy here the secrets of the Fang Gang.'

'Jonathan hasn't told me anything about the Fang Gang,' replied Troy. 'All I know is what Tiffany told me, that you're a group of young creatures from the dark side. It wasn't rocket

science to work out that Jonathan himself was a vampire or that you, Gory, shimmering your way into the Stoats' caravan, were a ghoul.'

Zeus barked excitedly.

'And, of course,' Troy went on, 'there can only be one reason why Zeus has taken such a shine to Scarlet. She's obviously a werewolf.'

Gory huffed and puffed, but he could see that Troy was telling the truth.

'In fact, they're probably related, sometime, way back,' reasoned Troy.

Zeus thumped his tail on the ground.

'I think Troy should be invited to the emergency meeting of the Fang Gang,' I said, quietly.

'What!' exclaimed Gory.

'It's only a few hours till the Party-in-the-Graveyard at Heemoglobin Castle,' I pointed out. 'Every vampire, ghoul and werewolf in Goolish will be there, unaware that a vampire-slaying competition is planned.'

'A what?' chorused Gory and Scarlet.

'I'll give you the full details later,' I said.

'Vampire-slaying competitions don't bother me,' said Gory with a shrug. 'I'm a ghoul.'

'If you're in the Fang Gang it's your job to help and protect all fellow members,' snapped Scarlet. 'Whether they're ghouls, zombies, vampires, werewolves or whatever.'

'And you might like to know,' said Troy, 'that the vampire slayers will be joined by a group of ghoul hunters.'

'Don't believe you,' sneered Gory.

Troy took a little sticky badge from his pocket and showed it to us. It read:

> ## Ghoul Hunters Say
> ## Be Cruel to a Ghoul Today!

Gory, who was pale at the best of times, went even paler.

Troy went on. 'And there are also a couple of former fox hunters, who, now that fox hunting has been banned, have decided to join Roderick, Vera and their vampire-slaying friends for a spot of werewolf hunting.'

Gory, Scarlet and I stood there in appalled silence.

Zeus was looking up at Scarlet and whimpering.

Chapter 14

'WE TAKE THEM all on, that's what we do!' declared Gory excitedly. 'The Fang Gang versus the vampire slayers, ghoul hunters and werewolf hunters!'

I shook my head. 'That would be a matter of six of us, if you include Troy –'

'Oh, include me,' said Troy.

'–And Zeus, versus, what thirty or forty of them, plus a TV crew.'

'You lot are a bunch of wimps! You just haven't got the stomach for a fight!' grumbled Gory.

'You won't have a stomach for a fight or anything else for that matter if half a dozen ghoul hunters get hold of you,' replied Scarlet, tersely.

'We need to warn everybody, so they'll be on their guard,' I said.

'We can't possibly get round every dark-side creature in Goolish,' Scarlet pointed out. 'There just isn't time.'

'Then we need to get back up to Heemoglobin Castle and at least warn your great-uncle and aunt and my grandad,' I told Scarlet.

'If they'll listen, that is,' sighed Scarlet. 'But how do we get back up there? It's late afternoon now. If we walk, it'll be dark by the time we get there. There must be someone who can give us a lift.'

'I know!' I exclaimed. 'Mort the undertaker! He can take us up there in his hearse.'

'Good idea!' agreed Scarlet. 'I'm sure Great-aunt Millie said he was bringing some gear up to the castle early for the Party-in-the-Graveyard, anyway.'

Scarlet rang Griselda and Crombie and told them both to meet us at Mort the undertaker's place and then we all started to make our way there.

'Jonathan?'

I turned and saw that Troy was standing on the pavement, with Zeus at his side.

'I'd better be getting back, or else I shall be missed. I'm only meant to be taking Zeus for a quick walk round the block.'

'Can't you come with us?' I asked him.

He shook his head. 'That would really arouse their suspicions.' He sighed, sadly. 'No, next time I see you I'll be with Tiffany Bliss, pretending that I'm looking for a vampire or two to slay.' He paused. 'Don't worry, it'll be all right.'

'Will it?' I wish I felt as confident as Troy sounded.

'Of course it will! You all have your special powers. And you will all be working together. Not only that, you've got a spy in the vampire slayers' camp.'

'Come on, Jonathan!' I heard Scarlet shout.

'Gotta go,' I said.

Troy nodded.

'Thanks for everything,' I said.

'Don't worry,' said Troy, 'you ain't seen nothing yet.'

'Grrr,' said Zeus.

When we reached Mort's, Crombie and Griselda were already waiting. Between us, we told them all everything.

'Hm, television, eh? I've always wanted to be on television,' said Mort.

'Mort, this is serious! Will you give us a lift up to Heemoglobin Castle?' asked Scarlet.

'Of course I will!' replied Mort. 'I've got a few bits and pieces to load into the hearse first. And, Jonathan,' he turned to me, 'I promised your grandfather I'd take his coffin up there for him, perhaps you'd pop down to

Drac's Cottage and get it out of the house ready. It'll save us time.'

I ran down to Drac's Cottage. When I reached the front gate I stopped. There in the road outside the cottage was a car: a very familiar car.

My dad's.

It could mean only one thing: Mum, Dad and Gran were back in England. Or to be more precise, they were inside Drac's Cottage, waiting to greet me and Grandad.

Chapter 15

MY FIRST INSTINCT was to charge up the front path, race inside and find them. I'd not seen them for months. I'd missed them all. There was so much I wanted to tell them!

Then I remembered why I was here: to collect Grandad's coffin. If it wasn't ready and waiting, Mort would knock at the door. Questions would be asked.

I doubled back along the lane to the corner of Grandad's garden. Then I squeezed through the hedge and, keeping my head down, made my way to the front of Drac's Cottage. There was a drainpipe at the end of the guttering. Feeling the comforting surge of vampire strength beginning to pump round my body, I leapt on to the water butt and began to shin up the drainpipe. I was level with Grandad's bedroom window when I heard voices below me. Looking down I saw Mum and Gran

walking down the front path towards the car.

Luckily they were so engrossed in their conversation they didn't see me. I stretched myself across to the window sill, forced the sash up and swung into grandad's bedroom. I saw his coffin lying still and shiny on the bedroom floor.

Standing above it was my dad.

'Jonathan?'

'Dad!'

I ran over and gave him a big hug. I was just

so pleased to see him. Then Dad took me by the shoulders and looked me steadily in the eye.

'So, you know all about your grandfather?' he said, nodding towards the coffin.

'Yes,' I replied. 'And it's all right —'

'It's not all right. I'm sorry, I should have told you years ago. I just never got round to it. But it's OK now. Your mum and I will take you straight home and you can put this nightmarish cottage and town out of your mind for ever.'

Dad's eyes were pleading with me and for just a moment I thought about grabbing his hand and dashing down the stairs to join Mum and Gran. I could jump in the car and be back at home with my mum and dad by bedtime, safe from the terrible dangers of the Goolish vampire-slaying competition.

'Jonathan?'

'No, Dad, I can't come home . . .' I said, quietly.

'Can't? Why not?' He looked at me. 'No! Not you, too, Jonathan? Surely, you're not turning into a –' he cried in alarm.

'I'm, er . . . helping with the Brownie camp,' I blurted out. Somehow I just couldn't bring myself to confirm what he already suspected: that I too was a vampire.

'Brownie camp?' repeated Dad in disbelief.

'Er . . . yes,' I babbled on, 'my friend Scarlet's great-aunt is Brown Howl, er . . . I mean Brown *Owl*.'

'Stuart!' my mum called from downstairs. 'Hurry up! We've got shopping to do!'

'Coming, dear!' called Dad, going towards the door.

'Look I don't quite understand what's going on,' he whispered, 'but whatever it is, it's not something your mum will understand. I'll see you later. OK?'

'OK, Dad!' I whispered. 'Thanks!'

From the window, I watched Mum and Dad walk down the front path to the car. The engine revved up and then they were off, speeding down the hill towards Goolish town centre.

I summoned up all my vampire strength again, hoisted Grandad's coffin on to my shoulders and trotted down the stairs to the hall, then out through the front door and down the garden path, just in time to see Mort and the others pulling up in the hearse.

As we strapped the coffin on to the roof, the afternoon sun was already sinking below the trees that covered the hilltops above Goolish.

We pulled away and it was only then that I remembered I hadn't asked my dad about the penguins.

Chapter 16

WHILE UNCLE MONTY helped the Brownies cook some disgusting goo made from flour and water, the rest of us put Great-aunt Millie and Grandad in the picture.

Grandad was particularly grumpy. He'd been there for three days now and *still* no one had needed a blood transfusion.

'No one's going to stop us having our

Party-in-the-Graveyard,' he said, stubbornly. 'It's an ancient vampire tradition!'

'We're talking about very experienced vampire slayers here,' Griselda told them. Like me, she was a vampire.

'Not to mention werewolf and ghoul hunters,' added Gory, with a shiver.

'Well, it's too late to call off the Party-in-the-Graveyard now,' Great-aunt Millie said. 'Some people will already be on their way.'

'I'm ready for these vampire slayers,' said Grandad. 'You couldn't get a more experienced vampire than me!'

I sighed. Grandad might be able to put up a fight for a bit, but once he'd had a couple of glasses of vintage blood anything could happen. I saw the rest of the Fang Gang shaking their heads, too.

'Don't you think you're a little bit old to be getting involved in fighting off vampire slayers?' asked Scarlet.

'Old? Old?' fumed Grandad.

'Mr Leech isn't old,' Great-aunt Millie said.

'He's ancient.' She paused. 'So, Scarlet, have you and your young friends in the Fang Gang got any ideas?'

'Er . . . no . . .' admitted Scarlet.

'I have,' piped up a small voice at my shoulder.

I looked round and saw Zliva.

'Me and Goblena have got a really *sweet* plan,' she said. 'It's called Operation Brownie.'

She flashed a toothy smile at me. 'It'll be brilliant, provided Jonathan can use his incredible superhuman strength and his amazing powers of turning into a bat and providing –'

'Yes, all right, all right,' muttered Scarlet. 'Just tell us what you have in mind . . .'

It was a cold, clear night and the full moon was beginning to rise into the starlit sky. One or two werewolf families had already bounded into the graveyard and a couple of ghouls were drifting about. A bat swooped down on to one of the tables, next to a plate of pizza slices.

'Griselda?' I called.

The bat spread its wings, which began to turn into arms and hands, and there before us was Griselda. It looked so easy, so natural. Would *I* ever be able to do that?

'I've had a good look round. Mrs Bliss and Tiffany have parked up in the caravan field. They're on their way down now! There are a couple of TV guys getting their stuff together.

The rest of the vampire slayers seem to be locking up their caravans.'

'Time to hide!' yelled Scarlet.

Every ghoul shimmered off, every vampire and werewolf leapt out of sight and the Brownies hid behind the tombstones.

Even from where we were hiding, behind the chapel ruins, we could hear Mrs Bliss's booming voice.

'Oh, look, poppet, they've got pizza and crisps. Shame it's going to be their last meal!

Now, we get out of the way behind one of these tombstones and wait for the evil creatures to appear. Have you got your stake and garlic ready?'

'Yes, Mummy!' whispered Tiffany.

Mrs Bliss and Tiffany crept towards the largest moss-covered tombstone. Suddenly, there was a terrible chorus of shrieking and wailing as out from behind other tombstones leapt a dozen or so Brownies.

Their banshee-like squeals would have sent me running, but Mrs Bliss and Tiffany stood there, frozen to the spot, as Brownie upon Brownie plastered them with plates of the flour and water goo they had been making with Great-uncle Monty. The white goo glistened in the moonlight, covering every inch of Mrs Bliss and Tiffany. They looked like ghouls.

'Eiiik!' screamed Tiffany. She *sounded* like a ghoul.

'Ooohhh!' wailed Mrs Bliss. She sounded like a ghoul, too.

As they began to move, globules of goo dripped from their arms like so much ecto-plasm.

'Camera! Action!' shouted a voice from the field, as the TV crew, cameras and mikes at the ready, ran down towards Mrs Bliss and Tiffany. 'It's a couple of wee ghosties!'

'There's our first prey!' yelled a ghoul hunter, running towards Mrs Bliss and Tiffany.

Behind them, I could see Vera Stoat urging Roderick, the werewolf hunters and the rest of the vampire slayers on. 'Come on, you slayers! Where there are ghouls; werewolves and vampires can't be far behind!' she cried.

At the gate to the castle chapel graveyard, Mrs Bliss and Tiffany, trying to get out, met the TV crew, the ghoul hunters, the werewolf hunters and the vampire slayers trying to get in.

There was a moment's silence as everybody got their breath back. And in that moment's silence there came the sound of knocking from a coffin that was standing up against the graveyard wall, next to the gate; Grandad's coffin.

Chapter 17

'LEAVE THESE GHOULS to the ghoul hunters!' screamed Vera. 'Roderick, give me that stake and hammer. If we get the lid off this coffin and get the vampire who's in it, we'll be well on our way to winning the Bliss Cup!'

Pushing the other vampire slayers out of the way, Vera and Roderick tore the lid off the coffin, while the ghoul hunters chased

101

Mrs Bliss and Tiffany around the graveyard.

'Out you come, you despicable creature of evil and darkness!' yelled Vera, raising her stake and hammer.

Out of the coffin stepped a penguin. Then another penguin. Then two baby penguins.

'Ooooo!' chorused the werewolf hunters and vampire slayers.

'Ahhhh!' cooed the ghoul hunters, suddenly distracted from their chasing of Tiffany and Mrs Bliss by the sight of the four penguins.

'Aaargh!' yelled Vera, who in her shock, had dropped her hammer on to her foot.

'Camera! Action!' yelled the TV director, as the penguins waddled through the gate and down the slope to the castle moat.

'How did those penguins get into your grandad's coffin?' Griselda whispered to me.

'It's a long story,' I began. 'You see, my mum and dad won this competition –'

Before I could get any further, a terrifying howl echoed round the night sky. It came from the direction of Heemoglobin Castle itself, just across the moat.

'That's Scarlet,' said Griselda. 'Time for Operation Brownie, Stage Two.'

I gulped. 'I don't think I can go through with this,' I mumbled.

'Of course you can! Just believe in yourself!' said Griselda. 'Everyone is relying on you, Jonathan!'

That didn't make me feel any better. I only hoped I could carry out my part of Operation Brownie successfully. If I couldn't, the consequences would be too terrible to think about.

Out from behind the chapel ruins bounded Griselda, in vampire form, snarling and flashing her fangs. She was nowhere near as scary as the Brownies had been with their flour and water, but she was scary enough. Over the graveyard wall she jumped, Gory shimmering after her. Crombie the Zombie followed, fixing the TV camera with the terrible glassy stare of the living dead.

'After them!' yelled Vera.

Pushing and shoving each other out of the way, werewolf hunters and vampire slayers chased after Griselda and Gory. Behind them ran Tiffany and Mrs Bliss, still being pursued by the ghoul hunters.

'Hey, man! What about me!' called Crombie. 'Aren't I scary?'

The truth was none of the vampire slayers, ghoul hunters or werewolf hunters were the slightest bit interested in zombies. So Crombie marched over to the food table and began tucking into the pizzas.

It was time for me to go.

I felt my fangs stretching the corners of my mouth open and small beads of saliva trickling down my chin. I was in full vampire form now. My part in Operation Brownie was this: I had to wait until all the vampire slayers, werewolf hunters and ghoul hunters were across the drawbridge and into the castle compound. Then I was to follow them across and, using my vampire strength, haul the drawbridge up and snap the chains in half so that there was no way out. Except for me, of

course. Using my vampire gifts, I was then to take on a bat form and flutter out through the grille above the drawbridge. Easy, except that I had never taken on that form before; not fully, at any rate.

As Griselda started to lead the vampire slayers, werewolf hunters and ghoul hunters over the drawbridge I heard Scarlet howl. This was wrong! She should have been away by now, out round the corner of the field! As I approached the drawbridge I saw the terrible danger she was in. She was still on the castle side of the drawbridge, right under the portcullis. Surrounding her were three werewolf hunters.

'Tally ho!' they called, as Scarlet howled.

Suddenly another howl echoed Scarlet's, and down the field pounded Zeus.

'Grab her, boy!' ordered one of the werewolf hunters.

But it wasn't Scarlet who Zeus grabbed, but the werewolf hunter: right in the fleshy bit of his leg. He let out an anguished howl, and then started hopping about on one leg. Zeus dealt with the other two werewolf hunters in the same way, before chasing them into the castle.

'Help! Mrs Stoat!' they yelled, as they raced off into the depths of the castle and out of sight.

I charged up to Scarlet. 'Run for it!' I yelled. 'I've got to get the drawbridge up!'

Scarlet whimpered and looked helplessly at me.

'Go!' I said. 'You've done your bit. It's up to me now!'

Scarlet nuzzled my hand and scampered off back over the drawbridge, Zeus bounding after her.

I turned back towards the castle and there stood Tiffany, brandishing a long, shining stake in one hand and a hammer in the other.

Chapter 18

I TURNED TO RUN, then slipped on the wooden drawbridge and fell to the ground. I looked up to see Tiffany leering down at me, her stake and hammer at the ready.

'Right, vampire boy, time to die,' she snarled.

As the stake came down towards my heart, I heard a cry and then I saw the gleaming stake fly through the air, out of Tiffany's grasp.

There was a splash as it landed in the moat below.

I spun over, got to my knees and looked up at Troy. He was behind Tiffany, holding her wrists. He tightened his grip on her right wrist and the hammer dropped into the moat.

'You wait, traitor!' she shrieked at Troy. 'I'm getting the others! There are plenty more stakes and hammers where this one came from, you know!' And, pulling herself free from Troy's grasp, she dashed into the castle.

Troy grinned at me. 'Hey, nice fangs!' he said. 'But what do we do now?'

'You get back over the moat, make sure Scarlet – and Zeus – are all right,' I said. 'I'll sort this out once and for all.'

As soon as Troy was off the drawbridge I began winding it up. I had no need to fear that my vampire strength had gone: it was racing through me with each turn of the winch. There was a clang as it shut to.

I pulled hard on the chain to snap it in half. Already, I could hear the excited voices of

Tiffany, her mum and Vera Stoat as they ran back down the stone stairs towards me. There was a satisfying clink as the chain broke.

There was no way out now. Unless I could think myself into bat form, I would be trapped inside a castle full of vampire slayers.

I squeezed my eyes tight. Nothing happened. The voices of the vampire slayers were getting closer and closer. I tried to think of myself as a vampire bat, but all I could feel were my hands and my fangs. I opened my eyes just in time to see a bat flitting towards me. It brushed my cheek, then perched on the metal grille above my head.

'Griselda?'

I shut my eyes and somehow knew from Griselda's touch how I must think myself into bat form. Suddenly, everything else just slipped from my mind.

I opened my eyes again.

'There he is!' screamed a voice. I saw Tiffany racing towards me, her mum close on her heels, wielding a stake.

I felt faint. I looked down at my legs and saw that they were disappearing, turning into nothing, like vapour from a kettle.

Tiffany thrust out her hands to grab me, but already I was out of her reach, gliding up towards the metal grille above the draw-bridge.

I perched next to Griselda, briefly, just to get my bearings, then both of us were away, swooping high and wide out through the grille, across the moat and the field, towards the Party-in-the-Graveyard: towards freedom.

Chapter 19

THE REST OF the Fang Gang, the Brownies, Grandad, Mort, Great-aunt Millie, Great-uncle Monty and all the other dark-side creatures looked up and waved. Griselda swooped down to the graveyard straight away, but I was enjoying myself. I did a couple of victory loop-the-loops and prepared to 'buzz' the food table.

It was then that I felt my wings growing, my

whole body expanding. I was turning back into vampire form! The heavier I became, the faster I fell, until I plummeted, like a rock, on to one of the food tables.

I must have knocked myself out, because when I opened my eyes everything was swimming around a bit. I could just see Grandad making his way towards me.

'Let me through, I'm a blood transfusion helper!' he shouted.

He thrust his face right in front of mine. He was grinning excitedly. 'And I think you need a blood transfusion, boy!' he declared.

'No, I don't!' I yelled, sitting bolt upright. I saw that I had split the table in two and I was in full vampire form again, with a bowl of jelly on my head and a bowl of trifle in my lap.

'Are you sure?' asked Grandad, disappointedly.

'Yes!' I told him.

'Grandad sighed. 'I don't know,' he grumbled. 'Three days as a blood transfusion helper and not one patient!'

Scarlet wasn't very sympathetic. 'Serves you right if your grandad *does* give you a blood transfusion,' she said. 'If you hadn't tried showing off, you would've landed nice and gracefully, like Griselda did.'

Behind Scarlet stood Troy, laughing his head off.

Zeus came up and licked me clean.

More and more dark-side creatures began turning up for the Party-in-the-Graveyard. Mort had brought his karaoke machine with him and Grandad was singing some 'lurve' songs.

Normally, this would have driven me – and everyone else – crazy, but as Scarlet said, at least it drowned out the screams and shrieks from the vampire slayers, werewolf hunters and ghoul hunters on the other side of the moat.

'What is going on over there?' I asked Grandad, when he took a break from singing to have a glass or two of blood.

'That is the sound of people being haunted by the ghost of Dr Heemoglobin, the mad dentist. He always floats about the castle at full moon.'

'Won't the ghoul hunters get him?'

'They wouldn't dare! He carries a dentist's drill in one hand and a giant pair of pliers in the other,' explained Grandad.

I shuddered.

'So, when will they be able to get out?'

'Later sometime,' said Grandad. 'Once the sun starts appearing on the horizon and we're all packed up and away, Mort or I will give the police a ring.'

I went and sat down with Troy and Zeus.

'Thanks, Troy,' I said. 'You know, for saving my life and that.'

Troy shrugged. 'That's OK.'

'What will you do now?'

'Oh, my parents are due home tomorrow,' said Troy.

'Yes, but you can hardly go back home with Vera and Roderick, can you?'

Troy shook his head. 'Something will turn up.'

Suddenly, Great-aunt Millie stood up on a chair and howled. Everyone went quiet.

'Fellow creatures of the dark side,' she announced. Then, turning to Troy and Zeus, she added, 'and friends.' Troy grinned. Zeus barked. 'I hope you can all hear me above the cries of horror coming from the castle. Tonight, at our annual Party-in-the-Graveyard we have to say a special thank you to a group of young dark-side creatures whose presence of mind and bravery has ensured our safety and our way of life. Werewolves, vampires, ghouls, zombies and others – please raise your glasses to THE FANG GANG!'

'The Fang Gang!' chorused everyone. We all lined up and took a bow.

Then Griselda stepped up beside Great-aunt Millie. 'But Operation Brownie would not have been possible without the Brownies!' she declared.

We all clapped the Brownies.

I found myself on my feet next to Griselda. I was shaking and almost as nervous as I'd been fighting Tiffany and the vampire slayers. 'And don't forget, everybody, we were all

saved in the nick of time by our friend from
the light side, Troy!'

We all clapped Troy. Then we all patted
Zeus.

After that, all sorts of creatures kept coming
up and congratulating us. I felt another slap on
my back and a voice behind me said: 'Well
done, Jonathan.'

I turned round to face my dad.

Chapter 20

'HOW LONG HAVE you been up here?' I asked Dad.

'Oh, sometime now,' he replied. 'You see I'd put the penguins in your grandad's coffin for a rest. They needed somewhere cosy and quiet after their long journey. When I realised the coffin – and the penguins – were missing, I guessed where they'd be. I knew where the Brownie camp was. It's been held in the same field up here ever since I was a youngster.'

'They seem very happy swimming about in the moat,' I said. 'They don't seem bothered by the noise at all.'

'No,' said Dad.

He looked at me, steadily. 'So, you've turned into a vampire, then, just like your grandad?'

'Dad, please!' I protested. 'I'm not a vampire *like* grandad. No two vampires are alike; any more than two people from the light side are alike. I'm a Jonathan Leech kind of vampire.'

'I did wonder,' said Dad, quietly.

'I kept quiet about it,' I said. 'I didn't mention it in my letters.'

'That's how I knew,' said Dad.

'So what happens now?' I asked.

'You may find this hard to believe,' sighed Dad, 'but your mother wants to move to Goolish.'

'What!'

'She thinks the penguins need to be near the sea. And she wants your gran to come and live with us; it means getting a bigger house.'

'Jonathan?'

I looked up into Scarlet's grinning face.

'Oh, Scarlet,' I muttered, 'er . . . this is my dad.'

'Hello, Mr Leech,' said Scarlet. She turned back to me. 'Well, come on,' she said, 'you two are the only creatures not dancing!'

She grabbed my hand in one silky paw and my dad's hand in the other and hauled us both out among the gravestones. As we danced, I caught my dad's eye. It seemed to me as if it was becoming sharper, more intense and piercing. I quickly turned away towards Scarlet. She gave me a big wink. 'If your dad wasn't so old,' she whispered in my ear, 'I reckon he could become a member of the Fang Gang, too.' When I turned back to him, he grinned, widely, so that I could see two small fangs resting comfortably on his bottom

lip. Being with dark-side creatures at such a great party seemed to have stirred the hidden vampire in him.

Luckily, by the time we got back to Drac's Cottage, Grandad's, Dad's and my fangs had all gone.

The sound of Grandad, Dad and me crashing about downstairs had woken Mum up. She gave me a big sloppy hug and said how wonderful it was to see me. Then she wiped her eyes, blew her nose and said I needed a haircut. She went back to bed then, but Dad and I sat up talking until dawn.

When Dad and I finally trudged up the stairs to my bedroom – he was sleeping on my floor, and Mum was sharing the sofa with Gran – Grandad was on the phone in the hall, ringing the police station.

A few minutes later I heard the sirens as the police cars made their way out of Goolish towards the imprisoned vampire slayers at Heemoglobin Castle.

Chapter 21

I SLEPT FOR A few hours and then got up. I still felt excited by the events of the night before. I went through to the kitchen. Gran was there.

'So, what's it like being a free woman, Gran?' I asked.

'Boring,' said Gran. 'But not for long. I had a long talk with your dad last night – or rather early this morning. He was telling me all about this Fang Gang you're in.'

'Oh yes?' I said.

'Yes. And I thought, that's what I need, a gang. So I've been on the phone this morning to a few old girls I met in prison and we're going to form ourselves into the *Gran Gang*!'

I groaned. 'And what are you going to do in this Gran Gang?' I asked.

I wished I hadn't.

'Oh, this and that,' replied Gran. 'Nothing legal, of course.'

Troy and Zeus had stayed the night with Great-aunt Millie and Great-uncle Monty. Dad and I went over there after breakfast. When Troy's mum and dad came to pick him up they vowed never to go on a teacher's conference and leave him with the Stoats again.

'There's no need to,' said Dad. 'If ever Troy – and Zeus – want a holiday, they're always welcome to come and stay with us in Goolish.'

When we got back to the cottage, Dad found a note from Mum on the kitchen table.

Fab news! Estate agent rang! He's found us a house! Apparently, a woman came in this morning and put it on the mkt. She wants an immediate sale!!! And guess who she is? That Belinda Bliss from the telly! Gone to see the solicitor! J

'Well, I never,' said Dad. 'Come on, son, let's take the penguins for a swim.'

Dad and I sat on the beach watching the penguins. I noticed he was running his finger around the side of his mouth.

'Er . . . these fang things,' he said. 'Will they appear again?'

'Yep. Next full moon,' I said.

'And this ability to turn yourself into a bat?'

I sucked in my breath. 'You have to be a really experienced vampire, perfectly at ease with what you are, to be able to do that,' I said.

'I see,' said Dad, with a frown.

'Don't worry,' I said. 'You're making very good progress.'

That evening I went up to the woods behind Goolish with Scarlet. We sat watching the sun sink over the sea, under the same tree, where we had sat, that first week in Goolish when I had discovered Scarlet practising how to howl.

'That was quite an amazing party last night,' she said.

I nodded. 'It's been quite an amazing last few months,' I replied. 'For me, at any rate.'

'Still things will quieten down a bit for you from now on. Now that you're settled in Goolish,' said Scarlet.

'Scarlet,' I said, 'I'm about to move into Tiffany's old house with my mum, four penguins, a gran who's the self-appointed leader of a group of old age pensioner criminals and a dad who's learning to be a vampire. Doesn't sound like a quiet life to me. I wouldn't put it past Tiffany not to leave some nasty surprises behind when she goes.'

'Still, at least she *is* going,' said Scarlet. 'No more worries from Little Miss Vampire Slayer.'

Maybe, I thought. But Tiffany wasn't the only vampire slayer in the world. As we'd found out at the Party-in-the-Graveyard, there were plenty more out there.

And they would be back. I had no doubt about that.

They'd be back . . .